The FLOWERS of TUMAINI

A Story Of Hope In A Season Of Despair

DEDICATION

To Mae Celeste Moomaw Jones, my paternal grandmother,
who taught me the importance of imagination.

To the millions of children worldwide who are
homeless due to the epidemic proportion of deadly diseases that have left them orphaned,
particularly seven young girls in Nairobi, Kenya.

ACKNOWLEDGEMENTS

To my husband, Charles, who supported my yearning to visit Africa and my preparation of this book.

For the many who always encourage my creativity, especially Cindi and Barbara.

To my son, Brian, a writer himself - for his editorial suggestions.

To Daland Webb for his technical support.

To my mission traveling companion, Lee Watenpaugh,
for sharing the experience and photographs.

And to my three creative granddaughters Jordan,
Nicole and Emily Jutras for assisting with illustrations!

Scripture quotations are taken from the Holy Bible, New Living Translation, copyright 1996.
Used by permission of Tyndale House Publishers, Inc., Wheaton, Illinois 60189. All rights reserved.

Copyright © 2010 by Martha Jones Ashton. 86674-ASHT
ISBN: Softcover   978-1-4535-8625-9

All rights reserved. No part of this book may be reproduced or transmitted in any form or by any means, electronic or mechanical, including photocopying, recording, or by any information storage and retrieval system, without permission in writing from the copyright owner.

This book was printed in the United States of America.

To order additional copies of this book, contact:
Xlibris Corporation
1-888-795-4274
www.Xlibris.com
Orders@Xlibris.com

In the beginning God created the heavens and the earth. Then God said, "Let us make people in our image, to be like ourselves." So God created people in His own image. He patterned them after himself; male and female He created them. They will be masters over all life. Then God looked over all He had made, and He saw that it was excellent in every way.

Long ago when people first inhabited the earth, life was good for both man and beast. God's creatures lived in harmony, respecting the food chain and the cycle of life. People lived off the land and valued the fruits of their labor. Human beings were fulfilling God's intention that they be caretakers of His planet

But over time many people began to focus on their own pleasures and to ignore the responsibilities put before them. They forgot their purpose for living. When man became preoccupied with material and physical desires to the neglect of God's beautiful Earth, disease and famine and idolatry began to consume the lands.

Alas, it came to pass that in one far off land many children were being orphaned because of the deterioration of the lives they once knew. They too suffered from hunger and grave illness. Many died either from neglect or starvation. One such child was Felicity, a young teen whose parents both succumbed to the dreaded disease that was fast becoming an epidemic. After her father died Felicity and her frail mother moved to a camp for displaced persons. Without any medical care, her mother soon became so weak that she lay on her mat all day. The distraught girl watched her beloved mother labor over each breath and then stop breathing altogether.

Even though Felicity knew that she was burdened with the disease that destroyed her family, she now had only herself to rely on. It was time to follow her heart. She longed to seek shelter from a world gone awry. She was convinced that a few people, even children, could make a positive difference.

Felicity draped a faded woven blanket over the back of her beloved donkey, Raffi, and filled an old plastic jug with water. What remained of her camp food rations was put in a burlap bag, which she hooked to the donkey's harness. Silently she bid farewell to the makeshift camp that had been her home for the past six months. Sadly no one seemed to notice as she rode off into the distance.

Felicity trudged along bumpy dirt roads in the hot sun, days passing without the sight of another human being. But she stayed her course, steadfastly believing that God would show her where to build a new life.

One afternoon as she wandered along the edge of a large savanna where the herds of wild animals migrated, a small pack of hungry hyenas threatened to attack. Their haunting barks sounded like laughter as they began stalking from just a few yards away. Felicity's heart was pounding as she quietly prayed to calm both herself and Raffi. She recalled having seen hyenas outrun zebra and other creatures larger than themselves to capture a good meal! Bravely the frightened girl continued to coax Raffi along for what seemed like a mile before she realized that the curious hyenas had lost interest!

Long hours passed into endless days of searing heat, persistent mosquitos, and gnawing hunger. Uncertainty began to creep into Felicity's mind. Was this dream of a new life just a desperate effort to escape her dismal reality? After a meager supply of dried bread and spicy rice was gone, wild berries and ginger root were usually the only foods available. The near empty old water jug slapped against Felicity's leg, as she rode atop Raffi's bony back. Just another reminder of constant thirst and never enough to eat.

Occasionally she and her lone companion would discover a long-abandoned well. Ignoring the knowledge that the water was no doubt contaminated, Felicity would refill the jug; and they would drink enough of the warm brown liquid to revive them for another day.

After what seemed like six or seven days of endless travel, Felicity's hope of a better life had all but faded. One night she lay upon the old woven blanket from the back of her donkey and gazed up at the multitude of stars. The lonely girl cried out to God to deliver her from her misery. As she wiped the tears from her dust-streaked face, Felicity gasped at the awesome sight of a large shooting star swooping down across the black sky!

"Oh, thank you, Abba God. You have heard my prayer and I am not alone!" Felicity fell into a deep restful sleep for the first time since her journey began.

The very next morning the weary girl and her donkey came upon a remote clearing on a hillside. The location appeared to be perfect for what Felicity had in mind. Situated at the foot of a large mountain, the grassy knoll was bisected by a stream of fresh water, babbling from the melting glaciers above.

Had it not been for the keen eye and sturdy legs of her thirsty donkey, the child may have wandered right past the heavenly spot, for it was completely surrounded by acacia and avocado trees, green tea plants and lush bougainvillea shrubs.

Felicity instinctively knew that God had called her to this place. It could become a haven from her country's ills, a place of solace for all those who might pass by! Overcome with joy, Felicity began to dance a little jig around her beloved donkey. Even Raffi appeared to be smiling!

A growling stomach soon reminded Felicity that it was time to gather some food. She tied Raffi up to a nearby tree and let him munch away on tea leaves and berries. Famished after a week or more of relentless travel with little nourishment, she first filled her empty stomach with samplings of strawberries and bananas that she could easily reach. While she was sharing a banana with Raffi, Felicity realized the tree to which Raffi was tethered was a mature avocado tree. It had been years since she had eaten the delicious green fruit! Without thinking twice she hoisted herself up the large tree by grabbing one limb after another until she could reach several ripe avocados. What a feast this would be!

After such an ample meal, Felicity began to feel very sleepy, so she lay down under the shade of some tea plants for a long summer nap.

It was late afternoon when Felicity awoke, but she energetically set about to begin constructing a shelter. She used thatching material and metal scraps that she had collected along the old country roads. From the nearby field she drug loose tree branches to the clearing.

Felicity may have been small in stature and ill of health, but her renewed strength provided the motivation to complete her new house in due time.

Refreshed after several days' rest and nourished by the fresh fruits that grew wild in abundance, the brown-skinned girl decided to clear a small area for a planting garden. Tucked away in her apron pocket were vegetable seeds that she had scavenged on her journey. With knees to earth Felicity prayed over the wee seeds as they were painstakingly dropped in the ground.

"Thank you, Lord, for your bounty.
Please provide harvest that will feed and sustain"

When her labor was done she saw that it was good, and she gave thanks to God for wisdom, strength and patience.

Miraculously the tiny rough-hewed field flourished with loving care, lots of sunshine, and sufficient rain. Felicity was very pleased with the variety of crops that began to sprout from the red dirt. Beans, potatoes, carrots and yams would soon fill the belly of the hungry girl who had put such faith in her Creator to build this heavenly sanctuary. There would be ample food to nourish her through the seasons to come! For a fleeting moment Felicity imagined her parents nodding their approval from heaven.

As summer turned to fall Felicity's humble sanctuary truly felt like a home. She was safe and blessed by beautiful surroundings. Even her health began to improve, thanks to all the nutritious food and clean air and lots of rest.

One day a large cow wandered up the hill and into her yard! Not knowing where it belonged, Felicity built a crude pen and welcomed "Maisy" to her family. Life was good, but occasionally Felicity did imagine how wonderful it would be to have other human beings share her home. Maybe they, too, would wander up the hill. . .

Then on the fortieth day in her garden of good and plenty, Felicity thought she heard singing from beyond the makeshift walls of her little retreat.

As she peered through the tea plants, her ears followed the melodious sound of young voices whistling the familiar Kiswahili song of her childhood. The lilting melody brought tears to her eyes, as Felicity recalled her mother cradling her to sleep with those tender words:

I thank you, thank you, Jesus
I thank you, Jesus, in my soul. . . .

There they were, six little girls in bedraggled clothes, joyfully hiking up the hill! The two oldest ones were supporting a crude makeshift stretcher between their shoulders, on which lay a frail child of about ten years. Felicity recognized the little girl's slow, labored breathing and fragile body as signs that she, too, carried the disease of her parents. Felicity slipped through the hedges and ran down the hill to meet this mighty band of misfit travelers.

"Jambo— I so hoped that you would come!" she squealed in delight.
"Welcome to Tumaini Gardens, home to all who seek respite from a plundered world", Felicity announced with a theatrical bow.

She escorted them back up the grassy slope and into her garden retreat.

"Let's get your friend settled on a cot, and I will prepare lunch for all of you. After your long journey, I know you must be exhausted."

As the girls gathered around the large log table that sat out in the yard, Felicity carried out generous bowls of steaming hot rice, chicken, potatoes, and vegetables in a juicy broth. A large platter of fresh fruit was already awaiting them.

"How could you possibly have known we were coming? There is so much food here–and meat! I love poultry!" exclaimed Jana, whose swollen belly revealed her history of malnutrition.

Felicity laughed gleefully, "I guess it is like the loaves and the fishes that time when Jesus was speaking to the crowds. There will always be enough. I have been expecting you – welcome home!"

As if on queue, the girls began to pray in unison:

"Heavenly Father, thank you for this most generous bounty that you have set before us. Surely goodness and mercy shall follow us all the days of our lives, until we dwell in the house of the Lord. Amen and thank you!"

Everyone was quiet as they munched on the first hot meal they'd had in days. Finally Chastity (a quiet child with a whisper of a voice) broke the silence by asking, "What does Tumaini Gardens mean?"

"Oh, I thought you knew. This is the garden of hope, for all who believe in a brighter tomorrow", explained Felicity. At that moment the tenacious young teen who ventured out on her own so many months ago realized that there had been a higher purpose in the longing of her heart.

Her hope and perseverance were not just for herself, but for all who were seeking to honor their Maker by restoring the world to a place of healthy balance for all living things.

"I've been thinking," Felicity shared, "that when I grow up, I'm going to be a doctor and make all of us well!"

Each child appeared to be caught up in her own musings, as the small group ate their stew and imagined what might be. In the security of this magical retreat, anything seemed possible! As the unity of this sisterhood became energized by the nourishing food and love of their young caregiver, the children began to relax. And in those moments of total serenity, a kaleidoscope of colorful images played in their fertile minds.

The selfless effort of just one person can profoundly affect many others. If that good turn gets passed on, like a ripple in the pond, then many more people will be helped. It only takes a moment to pass the love along! The whole concept of changing their world one step at a time so intrigued this little bouquet of flowers, that they went to sleep that night enveloped in hope and vision for a new dawn.

And so it was in Heaven that a band of guardian angels hummed a joyful tune as they scurried to report the happenings in one tiny garden on one eventful day on Earth.

God heard the news and knew that it was good.

And He smiled.

The Beginning!